For Pierson Broadwater—C.M.
For Bernadette and Matt—S.H.

Published in the United States by North-South Books Inc., New York.

Published simultaneously in Great Britain, Canada, Australia, and
New Zealand in 1997 by North-South Books, an imprint of
Nord-Süd Verlag AG, Gossau Zürich, Switzerland.

Library of Congress Cataloging-in-Publication Data
Masurel, Claire.
No, no, Titus! / Claire Masurel ; illustrated by Shari Halpern.
Summary: At first Titus the dog has trouble discovering exactly what his
job is on the farm, but then a fox's approach to the chicken coop helps him
understand how valuable he is.
[1. Dogs—Fiction. 2. Farm life—Fiction.] I. Halpern, Shari, ill. II. Title.
PZ7.M4239584No 1997 [E]—dc21 96-44501

A CIP catalogue record for this book is available from The British Library.

The artwork consists of collages made with several different types
of paper painted with acrylics and watercolors, pieces of fabric,
and color photocopies of pieces of fabric.
Designed by Marc Cheshire

ISBN 1-55858-725-X (TRADE BINDING)
1 3 5 7 9 TB 10 8 6 4 2
ISBN 1-55858-726-8 (LIBRARY BINDING)
1 3 5 7 9 LB 10 8 6 4 2
Printed in Belgium

For more information about our books, and the authors and artists
who create them, visit our web site: http://www.northsouth.com

Claire Masurel

No, No, Titus!

Illustrated by Shari Halpern

NORTH-SOUTH BOOKS / NEW YORK / LONDON

"Welcome to your new home, Titus," said the farmer.
"This farm needs a good dog!"
Titus wagged his tail. He wanted to be a good dog.
But what was a good dog supposed to do?

The farm was big and everyone was busy.

The school bus came down the road.
"HONK, HONK," went the school bus.
"WOOF, WOOF," barked Titus.
"No, no," said the children. "Dogs don't go to school!"

The farmer was plowing the fields.
"VROOM, VROOM," went the tractor.
"WOOF, WOOF," barked Titus.
"No, no," said the farmer. "Dogs don't drive tractors!"

The farmer's wife was milking.
"MOO, MOO," went the cow.
"WOOF, WOOF," barked Titus.
"No, no," said the cow. "Dogs don't give milk!"

The cat was chasing mice.
"MEOW, MEOW," went the cat.
"WOOF, WOOF," barked Titus.
"No, no," said the cat. "Dogs don't chase mice."

The chickens were laying eggs.
"CLUCK, CLUCK," went the chickens.
"WOOF, WOOF," barked Titus.
"No, no," said the chickens. "Dogs don't lay eggs."

Titus wanted to be a good farm dog.
But if dogs don't go to school, or drive tractors,
or give milk, or catch mice, or lay eggs . . .
what was Titus supposed to do?
He crawled into his doghouse and went to sleep.

Pitter, patter, pitter, patter.
Something was going to the chicken coop!
"WOOF, WOOF!" barked Titus.

The farmer came running.
"OH, NO!" shouted the farmer. "A FOX!"
"WOOF! WOOF! WOOF!" barked Titus as he chased
the fox across the field.

"YIP, YIP, YIP, YIP, YIP," cried the fox,
and it disappeared into the forest.

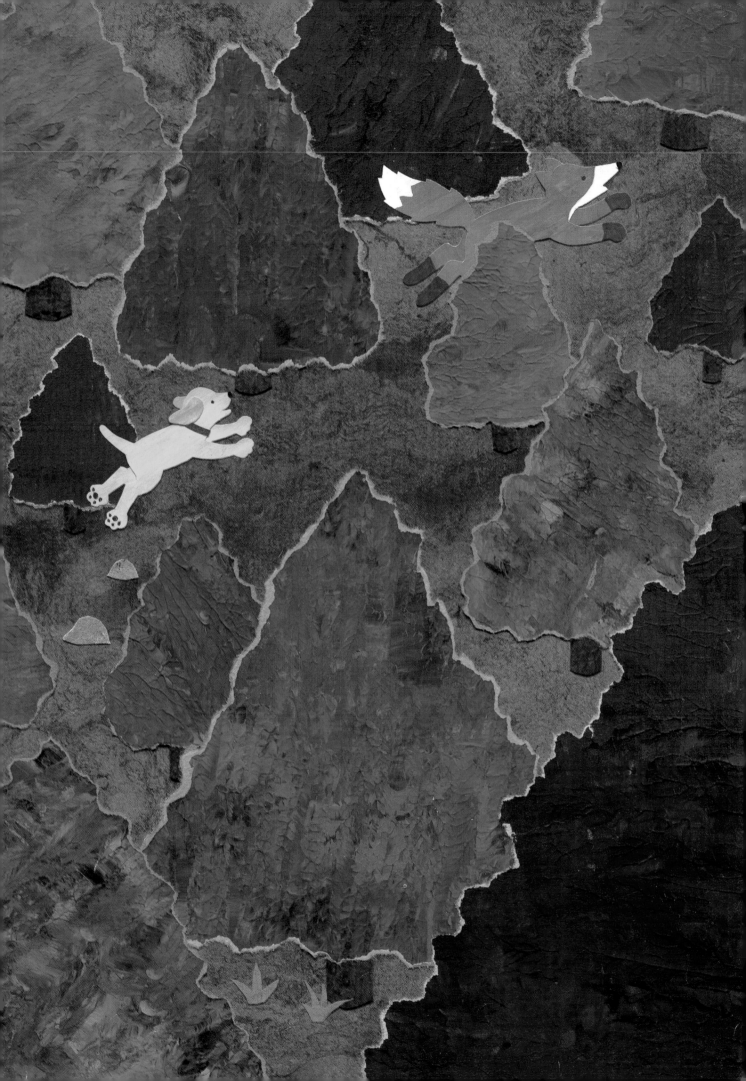

"HOORAY! HOORAY!" cheered the farmer,
his wife, the children, and all the animals.
"What a good watchdog!"
"WOOF, WOOF!" barked Titus. "WOOF! WOOF! WOOF!"